# JOY BEHAR

# SheetzuCacaPoopoo

## •MY KIND OF DOG•

illustrated by Gene Barretta

DUTTON CHILDREN'S BOOKS

To all the dogs I've loved before:
Pudgy, Phoebe, Molly, Gracie, Tallulah, and especially Max
J.B.

To Byron, for taking chances, and thank you to James Toogood
G.B.

Special thanks to Sarah L. Thomson

DUTTON CHILDREN'S BOOKS
A division of Penguin Young Readers Group
Published by the Penguin Group
Penguin Group (USA) Inc., 375 Hudson Street, New York, New York 10014, U.S.A. • Penguin Group
(Canada), 90 Eglinton Avenue East, Suite 700, Toronto, Ontario, Canada M4P 2Y3 (a division of
Pearson Penguin Canada Inc.) • Penguin Books Ltd, 80 Strand, London WC2R 0RL, England •
Penguin Ireland, 25 St Stephen's Green, Dublin 2, Ireland (a division of Penguin Books Ltd) • Penguin
Group (Australia), 250 Camberwell Road, Camberwell, Victoria 3124, Australia (a division of Pearson
Australia Group Pty Ltd) • Penguin Books India Pvt Ltd, 11 Community Centre, Panchsheel Park, New
Delhi—110 017 India • Penguin Group (NZ), Cnr Airborne and Rosedale Roads, Albany, Auckland 1310,
New Zealand (a division of Pearson New Zealand Ltd) • Penguin Books (South Africa) (Pty) Ltd, 24
Sturdee Avenue, Rosebank, Johannesburg 2196, South Africa • Penguin Books Ltd, Registered Offices:
80 Strand, London WC2R 0RL, England

Text copyright © 2006 by Joy Behar
Illustrations copyright © 2006 by Byron Preiss Visual Publications Inc. and Joy Behar

Library of Congress Cataloging-in-Publication Data available.

Published in the United States by Dutton Children's Books,
a division of Penguin Young Readers Group
345 Hudson Street, New York, New York 10014
www.penguin.com/youngreaders

Designed by Edie Weinberg
ISBN 0-525-47718-7
Manufactured in the USA • First Edition
3 5 7 9 10 8 6 4 2

When the puppy arrived at his home, he was so new that he didn't even have a name. But he did have round floppy ears, soft curly hair, and a long red tongue.

"Look, Mom!" said Evie. "He's part Shih Tzu, part cocker spaniel, and part poodle. He's a Sheetzucacapoopoo! Let's name him Max."

From the very first day. Max was a handful.

He was smart—like a poodle—and figured out how to get into his food between meals. He was spunky—like a Shih Tzu—and loved to bark at the birds outside the window.

And he was loving—like a cocker—and cuddled
with Evie all night long.

Evie sighed happily. "You're my kind of dog, Max."

When Evie got home from school, she was eager to
take Max for a walk. As soon as Max and Evie got into
the dog run, they saw a bunch of other dogs all being
walked by just one person. Max thought, *Gee, they must
have fun together.*

Max said to the big dog, "Let's play!" Her name was Remy, and she was a Saint Berdoodle, with love handles and drooly jowls. "Sorry, you're too little," said Remy. "I only play with big dogs—like me."

The little dog's name was Panchito, and he was a
Chihua-poo with tiny little legs and breath that smelled
like guacamole. But he didn't want to play with Max.
either. "You have round floppy ears." he said. "I like dogs
with triangle ears—like mine."

The tall dog was an Afghanoodle, and her name was
Angelina. She had long, flowing, swinging hair and legs
that never quit.

But she only wanted a friend with long, flowing hair like hers, not curly hair like Max's.

The other dogs were Petey the Peke-a-poo, Rocky the boxerdoodle, and Schultzy the schnoodle. But none of them wanted to play with Max, either. Max felt terrible. He wondered why they were so stuck-up. After all, he was a fun dog. They could have played sniff 'n' scratch, his favorite game. But nooooo . . .

Then Evie threw a bright red ball for Max to chase.

Max loved balls. He loved to chase balls, bounce balls, chew balls, and push balls. He even liked to hide his ball under the couch so he could force someone in his family to fetch it for him. He thought it would cheer him up to chase this one. He chased it all the way down the path. Unfortunately, he didn't see the hot dog cart until it was too late.

*Oh no!* thought Max, and then he had an idea.

"Lunchtime!" he barked.

Remy ate two hot dogs. Panchito caught one. Angelina got mustard in her bouffant, but she didn't even care. Petey, Rocky, and Schultzy chased hot dogs into the gutter, under the bushes, and between the legs of people walking by.

"You're my kind of dog," murmured Angelina, once she licked the mustard out of her hair. "You are definitely my kind of dog!"

"This is great," Panchito said to Max. "Mine even has peppers and onions on it."

"This is delicious," slobbered Remy. And all the other dogs joined in.

Max felt wonderful. Now he had all new friends to play with.

The next day, Max and Evie met his new friends at the park. The dogs played chase, chewed on sticks, and even dug a few holes together. Max was very happy.

Then a new pack of dogs walked by, and Max asked them to join in the fun. They didn't answer.

"Forget it, Max. They'll never play with us. Those are purebred dogs," whispered Panchito. "They have papers and everything. They're not like us. We're mixed breeds— part one kind of dog and part another. Sometimes they call us mutts."

"That is so wrong," said Max.

Evie threw a ball for Max. Max chased that ball all the way across the lawn . . . and right between the legs of the biggest purebred dog, a Great Dane named Hamlet. Max felt like he was under his dining room table.

"Stop there, small fry," said Hamlet. "What do you think you're doing?"

"Just trying to get out of the sun for a minute," said Max. "By the way, wanna play some ball?"

"Let's see, to play or not to play . . . Okay. I like to chase balls myself. You throw, I'll chase."

"Deal," said Max.

"What are you doing. Hamlet?" asked the purebred collie. Colleen. "You know we don't play with *that* kind of dog!"

"Grrrr." growled Max. Now he was mad.

"Come on. Max." said Panchito. "Those purebred dogs are snobs."

Hamlet nudged the ball sadly toward Max. "Maybe another day." he said.

This is silly! thought Max. We're all
dogs. aren't we? We have a lot in common.

We all like to chew bones . . .

. . . chase cats . . .

. . . bark at the mailman . . .

. . . and sniff poops.

Max decided to take matters into his own paws, so he snatched the bright red ball up in his teeth and jumped on a rock.

Max dropped the bright red ball. It rolled
down the face of the rock and bounced down the
grassy hill. It bounced over Panchito and sprang
right past Hamlet's nose.

"Get it!" barked Max.

For a second, Hamlet didn't know what to do—or not
to do. But he couldn't resist. He chased that ball across
the lawn, over rocks, through bushes, and under trees.

Then he caught it and nudged it
with his nose so that it rolled back
across the lawn toward Colleen.
"Get it!" barked Hamlet.

But before Colleen could catch the ball, Panchito
snatched it up from right under her nose and started
running toward Angelina.

He slipped on Remy's slobber before he
could get to her, and the ball went flying out
of his mouth.

Colleen caught the ball. Panchito tried to jump and snatch it right out of her jaws. Unfortunately his little legs were not built for a high jump.

Colleen couldn't stop laughing. and the ball slipped out of her mouth.

Now every dog in the park was chasing the ball.
Dogs ran and jumped and dug in bushes and tumbled
into one another.

They were running and playing so hard
you couldn't tell the difference between a cockapoo,
a schnoodle, a Labradoodle, or a King Charles spaniel.

It was a hilarious hullabaloo of hounds. Was it a
Yorkshire terrier or a whoodle? Was it a whippet or a
schnippet? No one knew. A dog named Jake jumped on
Angelina's back. She didn't even care that he mussed her
hair. Panchito crawled under Colleen's belly and made
her giggle even more. Petey sat on Hamlet's head. They
barked and yipped and giggled and laughed.

After a while, all the dogs had one thing in common.
They were tired and their tongues were hanging out.

"You're my kind of dog, Max!" said Hamlet.

"Mine, too!" said Panchito.

"Hooray for Max!" barked the dogs.

Max happily picked up his ball and wagged his tail
good-bye.